This Yael book belongs to:

{ .....The Brody's...................... ♡ ✿✿ ♡ }

Yael Worries No More

Published by Lite Girl Inc.

Text and illustrations Copyright 2014 by Lite Girl Inc.

www.bealitegirl.com

For updates, news, previews and special introductory offers on new exciting LITE Girl book releases and other products, sign up for FREE membership now at www.bealitegirl.com

Credits:
Illustrations and book design: Steve Pileggi/Blue Lion Designs
Cover Design: 3G Design
Editor: Tzippy Caton

Music and lyrics: Mattisyahu Brown
Vocalist: Rachel Ravitz
Audio Recording and Editing: Rachel Leah Reifer

Summary: Yael worries about just about everything, until she learns a beautiful way of letting go of her worries and becoming happy: Do your best and trust Hashem to do the rest!

Library of Congress Cataloging—978-0-9835231-3-0-51699
Printed and bound in China

עוז והדר לבושה ותשחק ליום אחרון

This book is dedicated in loving memory
Of our unforgettable

Mother, Grandmother and Great Grandmother

Mrs. Genendl Bas Rav Shlomo Berkowitz zt'l

Whose attributes, bravery, contentment, diligence, devotion, exertions, frugality,
gentleness, humaneness, love ,intelligence, modesty, perseverance, quiet demeanor,
righteousness, simplicity, sincerity, tenacity, uniqueness, work ethic and wisdom

Continues to inspire, motivate and energize our lives as we endeavor to walk in her
balanced path of דרך הממוצע

אשר היא דרך הישרה והיא דרך החכמים (רמב״ם הל׳ דעות:א)
עשות משפט ואהבת חסד והצנע לכת עם אלקך (מיכה ו:ח)

Avrohom Pinchas and Mindy Berkowitz., children & grandchildren עמו״ש

Yael was visiting Savta. Savta was singing to Yael while busily stitching her needlepoint.

"Stop!" said Yael worriedly. "What if the needle will poke you and make you bleed!"

"You're a born worrier!" Savta laughed.

You see, on most days, and most nights, Yael worried. It would begin in the morning, with the school bus wait.

"What if I missed the bus? What if the bus doesn't come?" Yael worried to her mother. "What if I'll be late to school?!"

"It's normal to worry a bit, Yael," Mommy would whisper.

"Everything will be ok. The bus will come soon, you'll see." But Yael didn't worry a bit. She worried **a lot.** She would fret and frown and worry, worry, worry until at last the bus would come.

The night before the school trip, Mommy began helping her pack.

Out came the snacks and the drink boxes. And sure enough, out
came Yael's worries.

"What if it rains tomorrow and we won't be able to go?" Yael worried
to her brother. "I've been waiting soo long for the trip!"

"Somebody's nervous!" David announced. "There goes Yael worrying again!"

"Hush, David," Mommy said. "It's normal to worry a bit."

But Yael didn't worry a bit. She worried **a lot.**

Bedtime arrived. Yael lay in bed for a very long time. She twisted and turned. And she **worried, worried, worried.** Over and over and over again, a voice in her head chimed, "What if it rains tomorrow?

"What if the rain ruins the trip?"

Sleep just wouldn't come! Yael went
out to try to sleep on the couch.

Abba noticed that Yael was upset.

"Why can't you sleep, Yael?"

"What if it rains!" Yael worried to her father. "What if we won't
be able to go on the trip tomorrow?"

"Yes!" Abba agreed. "That is definitely something to worry about. Yessiri! A **very big** worry!"

Yael smiled. Abba understood her worry!

"Come," said Abba softly. "I want to show you something outside on the porch."

Hand in hand, Abba and Yael walk out onto the porch, into the cold Fall night.

Yael looks up. The sky is very beautiful.

Like a million glittery diamonds spread out on a dark velvet blanket.

"Abba, look at the sky!" Yael whispers excitedly. "Abba, I see tons and tons of stars! Abba, how many stars are there in the sky?"

"More than I can count, Yael," Abba whispers back. "More than anyone can."

"Do you think Hashem knows how many there are?" asks Yael.

"Good Question, Yael," Abba says. His arms hug Yael's shoulders.

"Yes, Yael. Hashem knows how many there are! He counts the stars every night when He spreads them out in the evening sky. And then He counts them again at the end of every night, when he packs them away very carefully until the next night. Hashem even knows each star's name!"

"Imagine that!"

"Did you know, Yael, that Hashem also knows your name? There are billions of people in the world—like stars in the sky. Still, you have your own special place with Hashem, Yael. He worries about you, Yael, all day and all night."

"He really, really cares about you, Yael, because He loves you.
He always knows what you need. He wants you to try your best,
and then He'll help you with the rest."

"Remember, yesterday, for example, how we went to the store because
you needed a new set of colored pencils? Remember there was only
one left in the store? Do you know that Hashem kept it there for you?"

Yael felt a feeling prettier than the giant rainbow
she'd colored with the pencils.

"Remember, Sunday afternoon, when you were feeling so bored? You called Mindy. Her mother was taking her to the park and she said, 'Please! Join us!' See how Hashem helped you enjoy your Sunday afternoon?"

Yael felt a feeling happier than the happiness she felt on the carousel ride!

"So now that you're feeling worried, why not prepare your rain boots and raincoat for tomorrow, and then give the rest of your worry to Hashem.

You'll feel so much happier!"

Yael didn't say a word. She smiled a big smile up to Abba as they went back into the house. She also smiled a secret smile up past the velvety blanket of sky with all the glittery stars, up towards Hashem.

"Hashem," Yael whispered. "I have **a lot** of worries. Will you take them from me?" Quietly and happily, she went back to bed.

And from then on, Yael was different. It wasn't that she never worried any more. It's just that she did her best and was happy in her heart that Hashem would do the rest!

Here's the Be Happy song lyrics.
Hope you'll sing along!
And Remember, you can be a LITE Girl too!

(You can listen to the song being played
on the Yael Worries No More CD)

Hashem will take care of me
I am not alone
Hashem wants me to be happy
In my heart and in my bones

Hashem will take care of me
I am not alone
Hashem wants me to be happy
In my heart and in my bones
Lai lai..lai.lai.. la lay la lay lai lai..

How could I worry
When the one who created me
Loves me as His own
And gives me everything I need

How could I not just sing and clap
And dance joyfully
Just do your very best and
Let Hashem do the rest!
Lai lai..lai.lai.. la lay la lay lai lai.. clap! Clap!